From Tip to Toe

A Little Book of Fairy Fashion

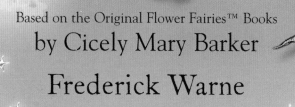

Based on the Original Flower Fairies™ Books
by Cicely Mary Barker

Frederick Warne

Dear Friend,

Close your eyes very tightly and make believe you are nose to nose with a Flower Fairy. What can you see? Now open them again. If you saw a beautiful creature who looks a little like you, only much much smaller, then you are on the right path.

What are the differences between you and a Flower Fairy?

✱ We have pointy ears
✱ We have beautiful wings
✱ We make our clothes out of the leaves, petals, pods and seeds of flowers.

Why are clothes and accessories
important to a Flower Fairy?
*They make it easy for us to hide
*They help us to do our jobs
*They help us look pretty for special occasions

What are the rules of Flower Fairy fashion?
*Everything we wear comes from the garden
*No two fairy outfits look the same
*No outfit is complete without a nice smile

Perhaps learning about the way we look
will help you to spot one of us!

Love,
The Flower Fairies

Hair and Hats

Fairies' Hair Care

Flower Fairies' hair twinkles in the sunshine and feels soft as dandelion fluff. They wash it in a glistening stream, untangle it with combs made from tiny twigs, and dry it in a puff of air.

Perhaps some of these fairies have hair like yours.

Long Hair

Long soft waves seem to dance in the breeze.

Plait long hair, leaving a few ringlets loose.

Short Hair

Tuck short hair behind pretty pointy ears.

Decorate with tiny petals.

Hair Accessories

Use a bright scarf for a stylish look.

String seeds together for a classic hairband.

Curls! Curls! Curls!

How we make perfect fairy curls:

1. Wind strands of wet hair round small twigs.
2. Hold in place with thick pieces of grass.
3. Allow hair to dry in a cool breeze.
4. Remove each twig carefully.
5. Shake head a few times for perfect curls!

Hats and All That

It's very important that a fairy's hat fits perfectly (because of all the flying!), and although an adult fairy's head will always be between the size of a hawthorn berry and an acorn, some fairies just won't sit still long enough for Sweet Pea to measure them!

Sweet Pea is measuring a baby for a bonnet.

Spiky helmets suit Tree-fairies.

Hats with wide brims keep the rain off.

Pretty caps for Meadow-fairies.

Scooped-out berries are a snug fit.

A garland of berries looks as good as jewels!

Fairy Outfits

Fairy-Tailor-Made

Flower Fairies are very particular about what they wear. Each outfit is designed around the special flower they have been chosen to watch over, which helps friends to spot them (including big people if you're very quiet!), but also makes it easy for them to hide when they need to.

All fairies design their own outfits, so no two outfits are ever the same. But it is Tansy who does the really hard work, because her cutting and stitching are the best in the fairies' Secret World. All she asks is that each fairy collects the material for their outfit.

Little flowers make perfect decorations.

Seeds for a hairband or buttons.

Pink petals for party dresses.

Cool green leaves for a winter skirt.

A Snip and a Stitch

Although Tansy does most of the sewing,
she has lots of willing helpers.

Pink uses tiny scissors to snip off
any rough edges or loose threads.

Shirley Poppy sprinkles fairy dust on every new outfit.
This stops the colours fading and
keeps the petals fresh forever.

Garden Clothes

Look at these beautiful clothes
that Tansy has made!

The Honeysuckle fairy sits
high on a branch. He is waiting for
Tansy to make him some shoes!

This little Flower Fairy's outfit keeps him well hidden in the garden.

These delicate wings took Tansy a long time to stitch.

The little Strawberry fairy has a very special outfit.

Party Dreams

Harebell's dress

Lavender's skirt

Narcissus' dress

Ragwort's dress

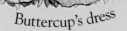

Columbine's dress

Buttercup's dress

Poppy's dress

The day after the Fairy Ball, the young Flower
Fairies love to see the beautiful dresses worn
the night before. They dream of the day they
will be old enough to wear such beautiful
gowns and dance all night at the ball.

Accessories

In the Bag

What do you think Flower Fairies might need
to carry with them? If you were to peek inside
a fairy's private purse, you might find:

My Diary

A little book for fairy notes and dreams.

Fairy dust.

Fairy coins.

Summer Fairy Ball.

An invitation to the Fairy Summer Ball!

Tip Tap Toe

If you had a peek inside a
Flower Fairy's wardrobe you
might find . . .

Summer
Sandals

Light and airy shoes for a hot summer.

These make every fairy light on her toes.

Dancing
Slippers

Special
Occasion

Flashy and dandy!

Winter
Boots

Boots keep tiny tootsies snug.

A
pretty pair
of fairy shoes can
finish off an outfit
perfectly, and there are
so many different styles
to choose from.

Wings to Flutter By

When Flower Fairies are first born, their wings are as delicate as cobwebs, but soon they become strong and colourful. Like snowflakes, each fairy's wings are different from the next, but all are sprinkled with magic. Early in the morning, wings glisten with dew, and the rising sun makes them reflect rainbow colours.

Dainty Pretty Things

Make-up

For special occasions, a fairy might add some colour to her cheeks and lips using squashed berries

Jewellery

Fairy jewels are made by stringing together buds, petals and berries.

Perfume

Every fairy has a natural scent from the flowers they look after, but all agree that these flowers make the best perfume:

Almond Blossom   Lavender   Forget-me-not   Buttercup   Sweet Pea

FREDERICK WARNE

Published by the Penguin Group
Penguin Books Ltd, 80 Strand, London WC2R 0RL, England
New York, Australia, Canada, India, New Zealand, South Africa

This edition first published by Frederick Warne 2004
1 3 5 7 9 10 8 6 4 2

ISBN 0 7232 49768

Printed in China